Timeless Tales FROM HALLMARK ™

RAPUNZEL

Adapted by Mary Packard from the original
TIMELESS TALES FROM HALLMARK™ story

LANDOLL'S
Ashland, Ohio 44805

A long time ago, in a faraway place, there lived a young married couple. The husband and wife loved each other very much, and they had a charming little house and plenty of food to eat. But they were not truly happy, for they did not have a child with whom to share their life and love.

After a time the wife became so unhappy that she stopped eating. Her rosy cheeks grew pale and her voice became weak. Soon she was unable to get out of bed.

"Please, darling," said her worried husband. "You must eat. Wasting away to nothing will not bring us a child."

"I'm sorry," said the wife sadly. "But I simply cannot."

Then one day, the wife noticed some fresh green rampion growing in a neighboring garden.

"Oh," she said, "it looks so good!"

When her husband brought her lunch, she refused to eat.

"Darling," he said, "isn't there anything that you'll eat?"

"Yes," she whispered. "I would eat a salad made with that fresh rampion from our neighbor's garden. I feel I must have it or I shall die."

"Then you will have some," promised the husband.

Unfortunately, the garden belonged to an evil old witch named Scarlotta. Nevertheless, the husband bravely leaped over the wall into her garden and stole some rampion for his wife.

His wife was overjoyed with the salad he made for her.

"Will there be rampion for dinner as well?" she asked hopefully.

"But, darling," he said, "you ate it all already."

"But I must have more," she said with big tears in her eyes. "Or I fear I shall not be able to live!"

That night the husband sneaked into the garden again. But this time he was caught by the evil witch.

"Well, well, what have we here?" Scarlotta cackled.

"Please, let me explain," the husband pleaded. "The greens are for my wife. Without them, she will surely die."

"All right," the witch said sweetly. "You may keep the rampion. In fact, you may have all you want," she said with a toothy smile. "But first let me tell you the price. If your wife has a child, I must have it for my own."

The husband was shocked to hear the witch's demand. But thinking that he and his wife could never have a child, he finally said "yes," so quietly that even the birds could hardly hear him.

Soon the wife regained her strength, and by autumn a miracle happened. The husband and wife became the parents of a beautiful baby girl.

"She's the child we've always wanted," said the wife, cradling the baby and kissing her gently.

Just then the door to their little house flew open, and Scarlotta entered the room.

"That child is mine!" shrieked the evil witch.

The wife held her baby tightly. "What are you talking about?" demanded the wife.

"You can't have her!" said the husband. "You'll never..."

The husband was not able to finish. For the wicked old witch had cast a spell on the couple that froze them in place. Then the old witch took the little baby from the wife's arms.

"You're mine now," she cackled. "I will name you 'Rapunzel,' another name for rampion."

Scarlotta turned toward the couple as she left the little house. "When you come out of your spell, you will remember nothing," she promised.

Scarlotta raised the child as her very own daughter, but she kept her high up in a tower, locked away from the rest of the world. The jealous old witch wanted Rapunzel's love all to herself.

Rapunzel spent long, lonely days in the tower. She wished there was some way to be free. Each day she looked out her window and sang beautiful songs. Her friends, the birds, felt very sorry for her.

And each day Scarlotta brought food and water. The witch would stand at the bottom of the tower and call:

Rapunzel, Rapunzel, let down your hair,
That I might climb the golden stair.

Rapunzel would throw down her long, golden hair for Scarlotta to climb into the tower.

Rapunzel did not like the tower. Each day was more dreary than the last.

"I would dearly love someone else to talk to," she told Scarlotta.

"I give you everything you need—food, clothes, a home," snapped Scarlotta. "What else could you want? You're mine, and mine alone— now and forever!" she screamed.

Rapunzel felt more lonely than ever.

One day, as Rapunzel gazed out the window and sang, a prince rode by and heard her beautiful voice.

"Do you hear that lovely song?" the prince asked his horse.

The next day the prince found himself looking toward the woods and humming Rapunzel's song.

"Come on," he said to his horse. "We're going to find out where that beautiful voice came from."

The prince rode through the woods until he came to the tower, where he saw Scarlotta and heard her call:

Rapunzel, Rapunzel, let down your hair,
That I might climb the golden stair.

The prince watched Scarlotta climb up Rapunzel's golden locks into the tower.

Later, when the witch climbed down and hobbled away, the prince imitated Scarlotta's chant.

Rapunzel let down her hair, and the prince quickly climbed up into the tower.

"Hello," he said softly.

Rapunzel was frightened when she saw it was not the witch. "Who are you?" she gasped.

"I heard you singing," he said kindly.

Rapunzel stared at him. "You must pardon me," she said shyly, "but I've never seen anyone but Scarlotta before."

"How can that be?" asked the prince.

"I've been alone in this room ever since I can remember," she explained. "Scarlotta, the witch, wants to keep me all to herself."

The prince told her all about himself and his kingdom. They talked all night long until they fell asleep in each other's arms.

Rapunzel woke as dawn began to break. "It's already morning," she said in a frightened voice. "You must leave before Scarlotta comes. But please come back tonight, after Scarlotta has left. Good-bye, my sweet prince."

"I'm not afraid of Scarlotta," the prince said bravely. "I'll only leave now if you promise to marry me."

"Marry you?" cried Rapunzel joyfully. "Oh, yes! I will marry you!"

Then the prince kissed her good-bye. "Until tonight," he said.

"Tonight," she repeated.

Just after the prince left, Scarlotta called up to Rapunzel.

"Oh, you take such foolish chances, my sweet!" said Rapunzel, throwing down her long hair. "What if Scarlotta were to come?"

"What indeed?" hissed Scarlotta as she climbed into the tower.

"Oh, no!" gasped Rapunzel. "Scarlotta!"

"That's right," cackled the witch. "Now then, who is 'your sweet'?"

"My prince!" cried Rapunzel. "He loves me, and he is going to marry me!"

Scarlotta took a large pair of shears out from under her cloak. "Marry, is it?" she said cruelly. "We'll see how much he loves you now!" And with that, she cut off Rapunzel's long, golden hair.

Rapunzel wept and wept. "I don't care what you do," she told Scarlotta. "This won't stop my beloved. He'll come to me somehow!"

"Maybe not," cackled Scarlotta as she took Rapunzel deep into the woods. "Let him find you here, you ungrateful wretch!"

"Nothing you do will stop my darling," cried Rapunzel.

"Then perhaps I'd best take care of your 'darling' as well!" said the witch.

That night, when the prince called, the wicked Scarlotta let down the hair she had cut from Rapunzel's head. The prince climbed into the tower—right into the witch's trap.

The prince gasped when he saw Scarlotta. "Where is Rapunzel?" he demanded.

"Your little bird has flown the coop," Scarlotta hissed. "But if you want to fly after her, you can." And, with a wave of her hand, she turned the prince into a bird.

The prince flew out the window. Day after day, the prince and Rapunzel searched for each other.

Finally, he heard her beautiful singing and flew to her side. When Rapunzel looked into the bird's eyes, she realized it was the prince.

"I knew Scarlotta couldn't keep us apart," she said.

"But we are apart," the prince answered sadly. "You are a beautiful girl. I am now a bird."

Tears filled Rapunzel's eyes. "As long as we are together and safe, I'll be happy," she said.

But when her tears fell on the prince, he turned back into a man. Love had conquered the witch's spell! The birds twittered with glee.

So the prince and Rapunzel returned happily to his castle, where a royal wedding was planned. The prince sent messengers to find Rapunzel's mother and father, and a huge celebration filled the castle. Everyone in the kingdom was overjoyed—everyone, that is, except the crotchety old Scarlotta, who still keeps a lovely garden of fresh rampion.

Copyright © 1989 Hallmark Licensing, Inc.
TIMELESS TALES FROM HALLMARK™ is a trademark of
Hallmark Licensing, Inc. used under license.

Manufactured in U.S.A.

First Edition 10 9 8 7 6 5 4 3 2
ISBN 1-56987-216-3

Prepared and Distributed by Landoll, Inc.
425 Orange St. • Ashland, Ohio 44805

Designed by Antler & Baldwin Design Group • Developed by Nancy Hall, Inc.
Illustrations by Vaccaro Associates, Inc. • Painted by Dennis Durrell